I Know I Can!

*Dream big +
be courageous!
J-NC*

written by **Veronica N. Chapman**   illustrated by **Daveia Odoi**

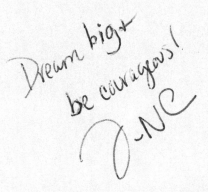

Acknowledgements

I Know I Can! is every bit a journey as it is a story. I will never forget that moment during my Spelman College graduation week when the words of the first draft sprang from my heart and onto the page—thank you, Spelman College, for the inspiration. And thank you, God, for the vision. To my parents, Gil and Idalene Chapman, you are two of the most awesome souls I know. I can't thank you enough for your love, support, and example. My family and friends are equally outstanding. Their support makes it so much easier for me to not only dream big, but also take action. Thank you, Daveia, for masterfully capturing my vision with your awesome illustrations. Paige, thank you for answering my call for a book designer, and for providing so much guidance and insight during this process. To my editors, Jonathan, Jash, Tapiwa, and Nina, thank you for lending your time, talents, and love to this publication. I, of course, owe an immense amount of gratitude to everyone who supported my publication campaigns. Thank you so much for helping me publish a book that will empower our little *Faiths* and bring joy to many.

Copyright 2015 © Veronica N. Chapman

ISBN-13: 978-1515162391

Edited by Jonathan S. Chapman, Jashonai Kemper-Payne,
Tapiwa Washington, Nina Katherine Elon Payne

Designed by Paige Davis

Published by Boxxout Enterprises.
Visit **MyCourageousFaith.com** to join the *I Know I Can!* community.

This book is dedicated to the following little *Faiths*:

Abigail Grace Jenkins

Adaeze Nwogbo

Adanna Nwogbo

Addison Monroe Jasper

Alaia Rolfe

Aleanna Marroquin

Alexa & Samara

Alexandria Rose

Alexandria T. Bright

Alexis Kendall Hobbs

Allison Lew

Amanee Miller

Amari Sourivong

Amber Hoey

Amber Rache'l Hobbs

Amina J. Fracyon

Amyre Jordan Hobbs

Anne Charlise (Charli) King

Annika Jackson

Aria Ashford

Aria Ella McCants

Arwen Denise Stanley

Aubrey Nicole Daniels

AutumnRose Burton

Azari Le Pouv

Brianna

Brooklyn Clarke Thomas

Brooklyn Summer Cheshire

Cameron Hickerson

Camryn Amira Saxon

Ceaira Gabrielle Dramani

Celeste

Chaiyelle Sims

Charlene (Big Faith)

Chelsee Wallington

Corrinne Marguerite

Daija Hurt

DaKayla Rucker

Deondra Lloyd-Heldore

Destiny Strawder

Ella Victoria Perille

Ellie Kirkman

Emani

Emily Toussaint

Gabrielle Allen

Gayla Jubilee Burton

Genevieve Neil Yarde

Gloryn E. Letlow

Hanniyah Edwards

Harper Renee Thomas

Iadonna Shakura Coleman

Isabelle Thomas

Jack & Oliver Blais

Jamera LaRae Baxter

Janae Turner

Jasmin Marshall

Jayla Marshall

Jazmin & Amaya

Jazmin Zora Grier

Jenia Curtis

Jordan A Mills

Journi Camille Dior Ashford

Karrington Lee-Louise

Keara Wallington

Kendall Nicole Martin

Kendra Woodward

Kennedi Marie Tolbert

Khloe Hudson

Kiemaria T. Jones

Kylie Aniyah Goode

Kyndall Harris

Laila Nichole Calixte

Lauren Lew

Lauren Pendarvis

Leia Soraiya Ema-Télé Olubusola Garber

Lillian Lew

Liyu Alnur

London Nicole Edwards

Lorissa Akins

Lyric

Madison Griffin

Major E. Muise

Makala Moyer

Makia Griffin

Mariah Moyer

Marleigh Butler

Maya Walsh

Maycee Porter

Micah Miller

Michael Sims

Michelle Eselean Harris

Mira Kieval

Miss Sunday Joy Baker

Morgan Elizabeth Lankford

My Princess

Mykhael Fant

Naima Sade' Curtis

Naomi Daleiah Short (my princess)

Nia Roberts

Nina Katherine Elon Payne

Rae-Madison Marguerite Hobbs

Ramah K.N. Austin

Rayna Lee Turk

Reagan Ellis Chism

Rhiannon

Rylee Shiah Roach

Samaya Lovett

Sanaya Miles

Sarah Toussaint

Sarai Dior

Saxon Family Girls

Serena Camille Hammie

Shar'Mane Serenity Janea Robinson

Shelby

Simone Evann Duncan

Skye Elizabeth Taylor

Sophia Alexis Brown

Summer Simone Sanders

Sydnee Bright

Symone Woods

Taniya Thigpen

TaNyah Summers

Tapiwa

Tatyana Flowers

The Jones Girls

Thia and Tiana

Veronica D. Garrett

Waverly R Alexander

Xiomara Castro

Xionne Edwards

Zamiyah M. Gonzalez

Zoey Ama

Zuri Alexandria Runnels

The world is yours.
Dream big.
Act with courage.
Lead with integrity.
Know that you are loved.

At the tender age of two, Mama said,

"Faith, with God, there's nothing you can't do."

And I believed her.

"The sky's the limit" is what Daddy would say when he'd tuck me in at night after a long school day.

So I believed I could touch the stars!

And in my dreams I did . . .

In my dreams, I did *everything*!

I visited the Louvre Museum in Paris, France . . .

I saw so many great paintings!
And everywhere I went people would say
"Bonjour!" That means "hello."

I strolled along the Malecón in Havana, Cuba . . .

There were people hanging out all along the sea wall.

One of them was a musician who played a song for me on his guitar.

After he finished playing, I said "gracias."

That means "thank you."

I embarked on a safari in South Africa . . .

The animals at
the game reserve
were amazing!

And I loved being the safari leader!

In another dream,
I got to meet with
Dr. Martin Luther King, Jr. . . . .

*Dr. King told me to continue the fight
for economic justice.*

I sang a duet with
Mahalia Jackson . . .

*Ms. Jackson told me to
use my voice to break
down barriers.*

I interviewed Fannie Lou Hamer . . .

Ms. Hamer told me to always stand up for my rights.

I even took a classical piano lesson
with Nina Simone!

Ms. Simone told me it's
a fact that I'm young,
gifted, and Black.

Yes, when I was a child I did it all . . .

Now that I'm older, I know it takes hard work to make *real* dreams come true.

And when it comes to your goals and dreams, don't let anyone tell you what you can't do.

Yes, there are challenges that I have faced.
But Mama always reminds me that
I've triumphed by God's grace.

So here we are on this beautiful day,
excited to see what will come our way.

Can you believe it, class? We are graduating
from high school today! And there are so
many great things I plan to do.

Because I know I can . . .

And you can too!

What can you do?

Everyone has special gifts and talents to offer the world.

And, even if there is something we don't know, we are never too young or too old to learn!

Talk to your friends and family about the things you know you can do.

Once you share your gifts and talents, discuss some of the things you want to learn.

Let's get started! I know I can . . .

The world is yours to explore.

Faith dreams of traveling the world so she can learn new languages, meet new people, and experience different cultures. Join Faith on her journey! Talk to your friends and family about the places you want to visit.

Here are some fun things you can do in preparation for foreign travel:

- Learn a foreign language
- Listen to music from around the world
- Learn about the different cultures in your neighborhood, state, and country
- Read about world cultures
- Try recipes from around the world

28404758R00015

Made in the USA
Middletown, DE
13 January 2016